Where Do MEDICINES Come From?

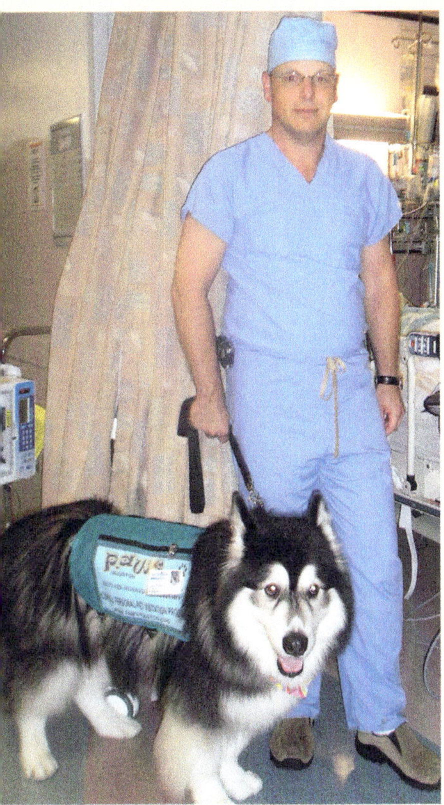

Dear Reader

The well-known saying, "laughter is the best medicine" is one that many people would identify with. We all feel better when we're laughing and having fun. In this book, you'll read about research confirming that laughter really is the best medicine. In Chapter 2, find out about an amazing organisation in Texas, the USA, that takes patients' dogs on hospital visits. Also, the Clown Doctors show how regular doses of laughter and fun in hospitals brighten up the days of patients.

> "WHEN SICK PEOPLE SEE THEIR OWN DOG OR CAT, THEIR FACES LIGHT UP, THE PAIN IS GONE AND THE SMILES ARE BRIGHT."
>
> DONNA DISHMAN, PAWS

You'll find out about where some well-known medicines, such as aspirin and penicillin, come from. We also feature some observant and clever scientists who have discovered medicines that have restored health to many millions of people.

I hope you enjoy the book.

Sharon Parsons

My sincere thanks to the following people for their time, information, images and enthusiasm for this book:

Donna Dishman, PAWS Houston, Texas, USA

Clown Doctors and The Humour Foundation, Sydney, Australia

NELSON
CENGAGE Learning™
For learning solutions, visit cengage.com.au

Contents

Where Do MEDICINES Come From?

1 Ancient Medicines

papyrus plants growing in the Nile River, Egypt, Africa

At the University of Leipzig, in Germany, there is an ancient Egyptian papyrus scroll called the "Ebers Papyrus". Written 3 500 years ago on the dried pulp of the papyrus reeds that lined the Nile River, the Ebers Papyrus is one of the earliest records of traditional medicines in the world.

Fully unrolled, the scroll is about 20 metres long. It contains chapters on many medical conditions, including intestinal disease, diseases caused by parasites, eye and skin problems, dental conditions and burns.

The scroll shows that the ancient Egyptians used a number of plants and other natural substances to prevent and treat illnesses and to maintain wellbeing. Among the 700 formulas and remedies outlined in the scroll are: a mixture of herbs that can be warmed on hot bricks to help alleviate the symptoms of asthma, a recipe for preparing clover, dates and oils to ease upset stomachs, and one section even prescribes half an onion mixed with the froth of fermented barley as a reliable remedy against death!

People all around the world have been using medicines in many forms for thousands of years.

Ancient India

In India, around 2 500 years ago, early writings on medicines appeared and were followed by the first encyclopedias about Ayurveda: the science of traditional Hindu medicine. Ayurveda, which is still practised today, uses hundreds of plant-based medicines, including spices such as cinnamon and cardamom, to cleanse the body.

cinnamon sticks

green cardamom pods (seeds)

Ancient China

In China, traditional medicines based largely on plants have been used for over 2 500 years. Chinese herbalists believe that illnesses are caused by an imbalance in one or more physical or spiritual influences within the body. To correct these imbalances, the Chinese combine herbs, minerals and animal parts to make natural medicines. Over 100 000 herbal remedies are listed in ancient Chinese medical writings. One of the most commonly used plants in Chinese medicine is the dried or fresh root of the ginseng plant.

a ginseng root

Indigenous Cultures

harakeke *flax pods from New Zealand*

Most indigenous cultures in Africa, North America, South America, the Pacific Islands and Australia developed their own systems of traditional medicine as well.

In New Zealand, traditional Māori medicines, or *rongoa*, were based around native plants such as *koromiko* (used for ulcers, sores, headaches, diarrhoea and dysentery), *harakeke* (used to disinfect and heal skin wounds and treat some stomach complaints) and *puriri* (for sore throats, backaches and muscle sprains).

The rainforests around the Amazon River in South America contain millions of species of plants, many of which have been used for years for medicinal purposes by the local indigenous people. Plants such as cashews, peppers, cacao beans and papaya are still commonly used. Nowadays, there is growing interest in traditional South American medicine, as the Amazon is an immensely biodiverse region. Based on the success of plant-based traditional medicines in different cultures around the world, there is much hope that many of the plants in the Amazon region could provide cures or treatments for many illnesses.

the Amazon River at Amazonia, Brazil, South America

2 Laughter As Medicine

Have you heard the saying that "laughter is the best medicine"? We know how great we feel after watching a funny TV show, or reading a book of jokes, or even just laughing for the sake of it with friends and family. In recent years, medical scientists and researchers have conducted various experiments in an attempt to prove that laughter is indeed good for our health.

Hehehehe!

Pets Are Good Medicine!

PAWS Houston in Texas, the USA, is a non-profit organisation that visits patients in hospitals with the patients' own dogs. Studies have shown that pets help to reduce stress and improve the health of their owners.

> "WE UNDERSTAND HOW IMPORTANT LOVING ANIMALS CAN BE TO THE HEALING OF THE HUMAN BODY AND MIND."
> PAWS HOUSTON

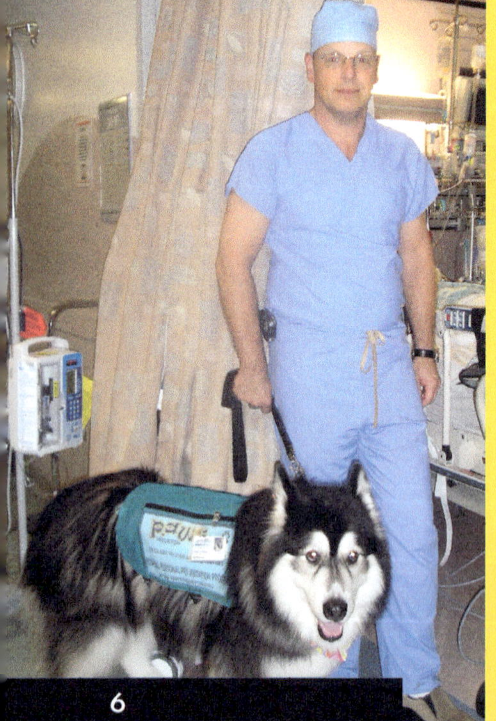

Doses of Laughter in Hospitals

In 2002, medical researchers in the USA discovered that laughter had a positive and healing effect on patients in children's hospitals. Laughter helped the children to relax and cope with the pain and discomfort associated with chronic illness.

The researchers began by asking 21 patients (aged 8–14 years) to place one hand in very cold water for as long as they could bear, while they watched a comedy. A second group of patients, or the control group, also placed their hand in very cold water, but did not watch a comedy at the same time. The research team observed that the children watching the comedy kept their hand submerged in the cold water for a longer period than those children not watching the comedy (the control group). Furthermore, the children who laughed the hardest were least affected by the cold. After the experiment, scientific tests of the comedy-watching patients' saliva revealed that their levels of stress had lowered, too.

Scientific Proof

In 2011, ten years of research revealed what physiological effects there are on the body when we laugh. A team of UK-based medical researchers uncovered proof that laughter acts just like a natural medicine. The researchers observed that people in groups who laughed heartily triggered heavier breathing, which then caused the body's muscles to relax. These physiological responses triggered a release of health-enhancing endorphins in the brain. Endorphins are chemicals that the body produces when we exercise, laugh, have a massage or eat certain foods, such as chocolate, strawberries, bananas and pasta. The endorphins help us to feel happier, less stressed and better able to manage feelings of physical discomfort.

If you are feeling unwell, try a fifteen-minute dose of watching a hilarious show to see if it improves how you feel. Medical researchers say it should make you feel at least 10 per cent better!

Clown Doctors and Elder Clowns from the Humour Foundation

The Humour Foundation is an Australian charity with teams of dedicated people, such as Clown Doctors and Elder Clowns, who work in healthcare facilities to promote and deliver the health benefits of humour. Clown Doctors based in children's hospitals have shown that their funny antics, presented with care and respect for patients, help make sick children feel better. There is a shared view among medical doctors, too, that patients generally feel less anxious about having surgery when the people looking after them in hospital show a sense of humour.

Clown Doctors deliver daily doses of humour to patients, staff and families at the Royal Children's Hospital in Melbourne, Australia.

The Elder Clowns work in aged-care facilities and geriatric wards in hospitals.

3 Healthy Foods and Fluids Are Medicinal

Open the door to your kitchen when it's stocked with healthy food and drink and you have access to your very own pharmacy! Because of all the research that has been done about what we eat, we now know more than ever about the value of making good food choices to maintain healthy bodies.

But, in a world of food technology, preservation and processing, food packaging labels today reveal that food producers use a lot of artificial preservatives and additives to make food taste better and last longer on shop shelves. In response to this change in food production, more people are educating themselves about the hidden ingredients in food, so they can make choices that best suit their family's health needs.

EAT YOUR VEGETABLES, FOR VITAMINS AND MINERALS AND TO PROVIDE HEALTH-ENHANCING NUTRIENTS.

EAT YOUR BAKED BEANS; THEY'RE A GREAT SOURCE OF FIBRE TO HELP MAINTAIN A HEALTHY BOWEL.

LIMIT YOUR INTAKE OF JUICE; WATER IS BETTER FOR MAINTAINING HYDRATION IN YOUR BODY. WATER MAKES UP ABOUT 75 PER CENT OF YOUR TOTAL BODY WEIGHT.

EAT YOUR MIXED SALAD FOR VITAMINS AND MINERALS, CARBOHYDRATES AND FIBRE!

SPREAD HONEY ON YOUR TOAST, IT IS A GREAT SOURCE OF ENZYMES, MINERALS, VITAMINS AND ANTIOXIDANTS.
HONEY
EAT YOUR RICE SALAD; IT'S A GOOD SOURCE OF CARBOHYDRATES FOR ENERGY, ESPECIALLY IF MADE WITH BROWN RICE!
EAT YOUR FISH; IT'S A GOOD SOURCE OF PROTEIN TO BUILD AND REPAIR YOUR MUSCLES AND BONES.
A SANDWICH IS AN IDEAL WAY TO GET FATS, PROTEIN, SALAD AND CARBOHYDRATES ALL IN ONE GO!
EAT YOUR FRESH FRUIT SALAD, FOR VITAMINS, MINERALS, FIBRE AND WATER.

4 Bush Food for Breakfast!

TEXT TYPE
Response

Last night, I watched a documentary called *Bush Food for Breakfast*, about a family who have continued a long tradition of growing vegetables, gathering food from the bush and hunting for eggs laid by their free-range chickens. The program was really useful! My latest school project is called, "Gathering and Growing Food". At school this past week, we learnt about the history of hunter and gatherer cultures to provide us with background information for the project. Our teacher has asked our class to write about people in today's world who, just like the people in the documentary, gather and grow food to sustain their families.

coastline in the North Island of New Zealand

A Relevant Documentary

I could really identify with the program because the presenters, Kiri and Tane, were a brother and a sister, about my age, who went for a holiday to their grandparents' farm in New Zealand. I have grandparents living in New Zealand, too, so the program really captured my attention. I live in Perth, Western Australia, and I have never travelled to New Zealand, so I enjoyed seeing what my grandparents' country looks like. Watching a documentary that was relevant to my life was really interesting, and it will help me write a more meaningful project.

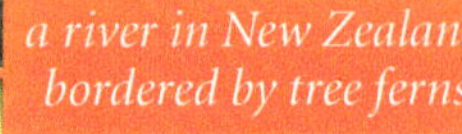

a river in New Zealand bordered by tree ferns

An Informative Narration

The camera followed Kiri and Tane during their first morning at the farm, and their narration made me feel like I was right there. Tane said that it's a tradition in their family to help their grandparents make *kai* for breakfast. I didn't know what *kai* was, but I thought they would probably go to the kitchen to make it. Instead, they went outside to the vegetable garden! There, they picked peas, spring onions and tomatoes, and had fun searching for eggs laid by their free-range hens.

Then Kiri said that *kai* means food in the Māori language, and that they were collecting ingredients from outside. She said, "I'm going to dig around the garden for kumara, which is a traditional Māori sweet potato. When I feel its bulbous shape in the dirt it's like finding treasure!" When she proudly held up a kumara it reminded me of the fun I've had digging up potatoes from our garden.

Spring Onions

Nutrition: Spring onions are a highly nutritious vegetable, with high levels of vitamin K for bone health.

Peas

Nutrition: Fresh peas are one of the most nutritious of the legume vegetables. They are high in essential minerals, vitamins and antioxidants.

Sweet Potatoes

Nutrition: In New Zealand, the sweet potato is called a kumara. It is high in many nutrients, such as iron and calcium, and vitamins A and C.

Tomatoes

Nutrition: Tomatoes provide a range of nutrients and one of the most beneficial is lycopene. Medical studies report that lycopene can help prevent cancer.

Free-Range Chicken Eggs

Nutrition: Studies show that chickens that feed on farm pastures lay eggs with higher levels of nutrition than caged chickens.

Bush Food for Breakfast! continues on pages 14–15

Safe-to-Eat Bush Foods

Throughout the documentary, Kiri and Tane learned about bush foods and traditional Māori foods, and I did, too. Kiri said, "It's really cool to learn which plants we can eat from the bush without getting sick!" I certainly agree with that!

After finding ingredients in the garden, the kids followed their grandparents into the bushland behind the house. Tane explained that they were looking for some edible fern fronds, known as bush asparagus, or by their Māori name, *piko piko*. He warned that it's important to properly identify an edible fern because there are only a few species that are safe to eat out of about 230 ferns growing in New Zealand. His grandmother told him that *piko piko* from the *mamaku*, or black tree fern, are safe to eat. Then she pointed out some flowers that can help with a sore throat! She told Tane that she had learned all about natural food and medicine from her grandmother.

MOST WILD FERNS ARE POISONOUS

Fern fronds from about seven ferns are safe to eat. Fern fronds are coiled in a tight spiral formation, and they are called *piko piko* or *koru* in Māori.

a tree fern canopy in the New Zealand bush

Edible Fern Fronds

The Māori fern frond *piko piko* is also known as bush asparagus. It is highly nutritious and is used by some New Zealand chefs in cooking.

Sow Thistle

Nutrition: *Puha* is the Māori name for the sow thistle. Its leaves are high in many vitamins and minerals, such as vitamins A and C, and calcium and iron.

A Delicious Finale

Finally, they all went back to the house to make their breakfast and talk about all the plants they had seen. Soon they had made a delicious-looking omelette and some kumara wedges. That was the one thing I didn't enjoy about the program: I couldn't smell or taste the amazing food! After everyone finished eating, Kiri thanked her grandparents and said that she and Tane felt privileged to have learned so much information from their elders about which bush foods and medicines could keep them healthy. She promised that she and Tane would pass their knowledge of traditional bush foods on to the next generation when it was their turn. I think that made their grandparents really happy.

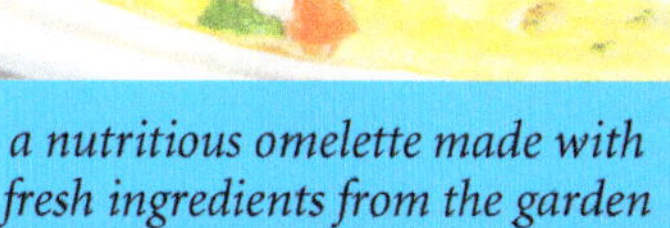

a nutritious omelette made with fresh ingredients from the garden

That's me, writing my project outside in our backyard.

wedges of kumara (sweet potato)

An Inspirational Program

As I switched off the TV, I realised that my notepad was completely full. I had pages and pages of information for my project! I felt inspired by the documentary to find out more about the uses of bush food. As a result of what I'd learnt from the program, and from researching on the internet, I found that many plants around the world can be used as food, medicine, building materials and a lot of other things, too! And that's how my project is going to begin: "For centuries my Māori ancestors survived well by using the plants they found in their natural environment for food and medicines. Today, we can incorporate aspects of their gathering and growing traditions into our lifestyle, regardless of where we live in the world."

5 Moulds Can Be Medicines

> … PENICILLIN STARTED AS A CHANCE OBSERVATION …
> ALEXANDER FLEMING, NOBEL LECTURE, 1945

The power of observation can result in life-changing discoveries, as Alexander Fleming found out in his laboratory in 1928. He discovered, quite by accident, that certain moulds, like penicillin, could fight bad bacteria!

Fleming found mould in a culture plate that was part of a failed experiment. He observed that no bacteria existed around the mould that had accidentally found its way onto the culture plate, so he decided to investigate it. By isolating the mould onto its own culture plate, he discovered that the mould released a substance that prevented the growth of bacteria. As it belonged to a genus of mould fungi called *Penicillium*, Fleming named the substance penicillin. Mould growing on the culture plate had prevented the growth of bacteria.

In those days, bacterial infection was feared. As a bacteriologist, Alexander Fleming was already searching for cures for bacteria-related illnesses, so he understood how important his discovery was!

Alexander Fleming

History

Fleming's Discovery in Tears!

Alexander Fleming was first to discover that an antibacterial enzyme exists in tears, nasal mucus and in egg whites. In 1922, Fleming discovered that the enzyme, called lysozyme, quickly broke down certain bacteria. Today, lysozyme is used in many antibacterial functions, including food preservation.

Fleming said that it was the discovery of lysozyme that assisted him in his investigations into how penicillin worked to kill more dangerous bacteria.

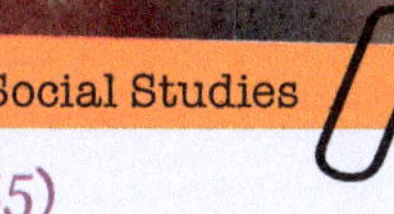

Alexander Fleming (1881–1955)

Alexander Fleming was born into a Scottish farming family on 6 August 1881. He graduated from university as a physician and chose to specialise in bacteriology. Today he is world-famous for his work in the field of antibacterial discoveries, including, in 1928, his most significant, penicillin. He also worked for the Royal Army Medical Corps where he made a number of discoveries about the use of antiseptics. He was knighted in 1944, and became Sir Alexander Fleming.

mould grows on a decaying orange

MOULD AND ALLERGIES

Moulds are fungi that thrive in warm or moist places, such as on food kept in storage for too long. Many people are allergic to mould when it is left to grow on moist surfaces in homes.

How Does Penicillin Work?

Penicillin treats infections caused by bacteria. It kills the bacteria and prevents their cell walls from growing and dividing into more bacteria. The bacteria die when their cell walls weaken. Today, there are different kinds of penicillin and it is administered in various forms: injection, intravenously (drip), tablet, capsule, syrup and solution.

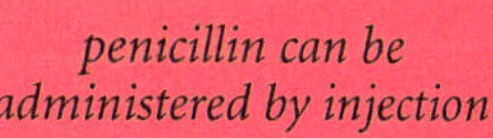
penicillin can be administered by injection

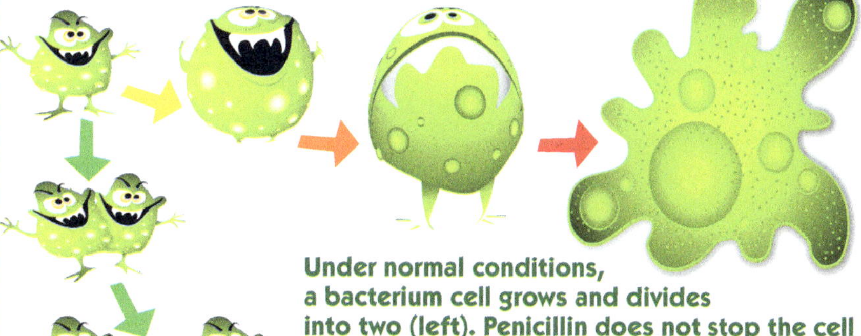

How Does Penicillin Work?

Under normal conditions, a bacterium cell grows and divides into two (left). Penicillin does not stop the cell from growing, but prevents it from dividing (above). Eventually, the cell wall becomes too stretched and weak and the bacterium bursts.

ALLERGIC TO PENICILLIN

Some people are allergic to penicillin, so it's wise to monitor how your body feels after your first dose of penicillin or other antibiotics.

Penicillin Problem for Fleming

Fleming's discovery wasn't accepted by the medical profession straight away, because he also found that penicillin was easily destroyed. He couldn't work out how to make it more stable, and so he (and other bacteriologists) couldn't properly test penicillin in clinical trials.

From Fleming to Florey

Fleming published his findings despite the problems with stability. This prompted a medical team, led by Howard Florey and Ernst B. Chain, to continue working with the penicillin mould from 1939 into the 1940s.

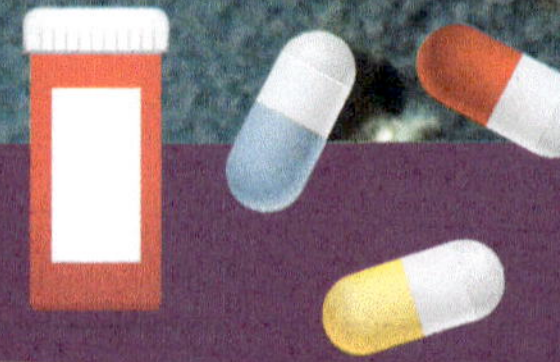

> "THEY (FLOREY AND CHAIN) OBTAINED MY STRAIN OF *PENICILLIN NOTATUM* AND SUCCEEDED IN CONCENTRATING PENICILLIN WITH THE RESULT THAT WE NOW HAVE CONCENTRATED PENICILLIN WHICH IS ACTIVE BEYOND THE WILDEST DREAMS I COULD POSSIBLY HAVE HAD IN THOSE EARLY DAYS."
>
> ALEXANDER FLEMING, 1945

Howard Florey

Florey and Chain Advance Penicillin

In 1938, Australian scientists Howard Florey and Ernst B. Chain organised a group of scientists to work together as a team in the UK. This was an innovative idea as it was not normal for scientists to work in teams in those days. Their task was to investigate antibacterial substances that were produced by mould. In doing so, they came across Alexander Fleming's report on penicillin and decided to find out more about it.

Social Studies

Howard Florey (1898–1968)

Sir Howard Florey was born in Adelaide, South Australia. In 1924, after graduating from Adelaide University, he was awarded a scholarship for further study and work in the UK. In 1944, he was awarded the honour of Knight Bachelor for his work with penicillin.

Ernst B. Chain

Social Studies

Ernst B. Chain (1906–1979)

Ernst B. Chain was born in Germany and as a chemist (and industrialist) he is credited for his work in identifying the chemical structure of penicillin. He worked as part of Howard Florey's team on the antibacterial nature of the mould containing penicillin. He worked on snake venoms, too!

Penicillin Starts Small

By 1939, Florey's team were able to manufacture small quantities of penicillin in a form that had proven to be successful in treating bacteria-related illnesses.

A Weekend Experiment

In the 1940s, soon after World War II had begun, the problem of finding an effective form of combating bacteria had become urgent. The first trials to find out if the penicillin could kill bacteria were conducted on a group of mice. Howard Florey's team injected a life-threatening dose of bacteria into eight mice and then injected penicillin into four out of the eight mice. The next day, the four mice injected with penicillin were still alive but the untreated mice had died.

Wartime Production of Penicillin

With government assistance their work enabled larger production of penicillin, which was used to treat soldiers' war wounds. From mid-1944, soldiers fighting for the Allied countries were being treated with penicillin and many believe that it helped the Allied countries to win the war. (Allied countries included the UK, the USA, Australia, New Zealand, Canada, France, Russia – formerly called the Union of Soviet Socialist Republics – South Africa, China and Greece.)

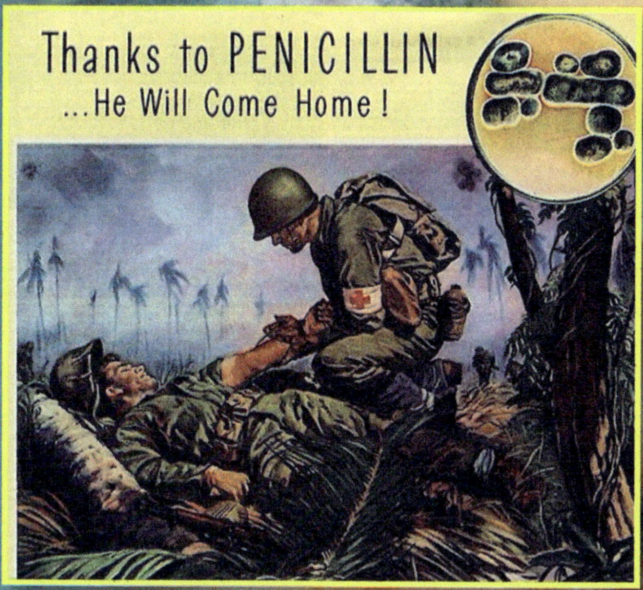

Nobel Prize in 1945

Fleming recalled observing in 1945 the large-scale production of mould in giant aerated tanks. He felt a sense of satisfaction that this all began with his discovery of mould growing on a small culture plate.

Sir Alexander Fleming, Sir Howard Florey and Ernst B. Chain were successful in stabilising and testing the mould, and they shared the Nobel Prize in Physiology or Medicine in 1945 for their discovery of penicillin and its ability to fight many infectious diseases.

Why was this a significant moment in the history of medicine?

Penicillin became the first antibiotic to successfully treat serious infections, resulting in the saving of millions of lives. Because of this, its use is considered to have been one of the greatest developments ever made in medicine.

Aspirin Made from Trees

Aspirin is one of the most widely consumed forms of over-the-counter medicine in the world. There are many uses for aspirin: the relief of mild to moderate pain; reducing fever; headaches; cold- or flu-like symptoms, and inflammation due to sports injuries.

Aspirin Extracted from Tree Bark

In simple terms, aspirin was first made using salacin, a compound that can be extracted from the bark of trees, such as the white willow, birch and poplar. The salacin was then converted to salicylic acid and later processed to form acetylsalicylic acid, which is the active ingredient in aspirin.

First Aid Before Taking Aspirin

Before taking any pain-relieving medicine such as aspirin, consider whether first-aid measures may be effective.

First Aid for Headaches

Sometimes a headache can be a symptom of dehydration, so before reaching for an aspirin, first try drinking a big glass of water.

First Aid for Colds and Flu

Sometimes it may be possible to reduce the duration of a cold by including foods high in vitamin C, such as garlic and ginger, with meals. A warm drink of lemon juice and honey can help you to feel better, too.

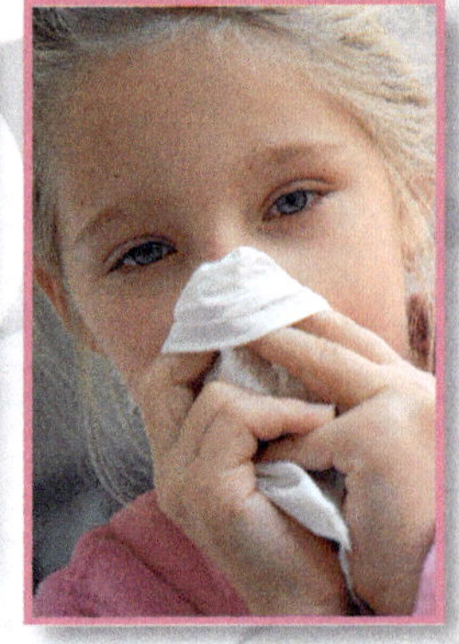

First Aid for Sports Injuries

Sometimes it may be helpful to visit a doctor or a physiotherapist before using medicine to self-treat inflammation from sports injuries.

a weeping willow tree

a birch tree

Aspirin at the Pharmacy

To help people choose the right aspirin at the pharmacy, aspirin is available in varying strengths. It is wise to first read the directions on the package, but your doctor will always provide the best advice.

aspirin being made inside a manufacturing facility

HOW ASPIRIN REDUCES PAIN

Aspirin works to relieve pain by minimising the nerve sensations at the origin of the pain and in the body's central nervous system.

Chemistry of Aspirin

The chemical process to make raw aspirin combines salicylic acid with acetic anhydride to form acetylsalicylic acid (aspirin) and acetic acid. This is the process that occurs before the raw aspirin is combined with other ingredients to make tablets and capsules. Some inactive ingredients that have been used to help bind the raw aspirin into tablet form are carnauba wax (derived from leaf wax on certain palm trees), cornstarch (starch from corn grains) and powdered cellulose (extracted from certain fruits and vegetables).

The chemical formula for aspirin is $C_9H_8O_4$. Its molecular structure is shown to the right.

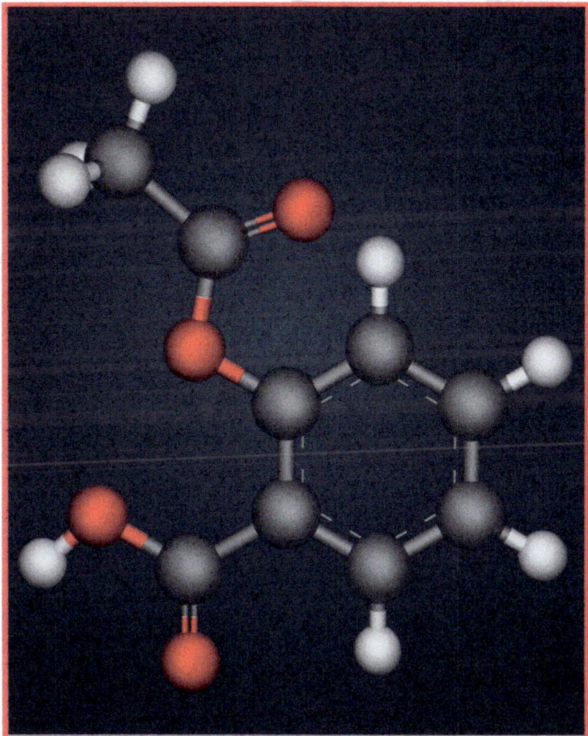

Black: shows nine carbon molecules

Grey: shows eight hydrogen molecules

Red: shows four oxygen molecules

Aspirin, Then and Now

Who Discovered Aspirin?

In 1897, Felix Hoffmann, a chemist who worked for a German pharmaceutical company, was credited with being the first to create aspirin, or acetylsalicylic acid. Hoffman's father suffered from rheumatoid arthritis and consumed salicylic acid to relieve the pain. In this pure form, the salicylic acid had an unpleasant taste and many side effects, like stomach irritation and nausea.

Early Trials of Aspirin Powder

In 1899, doctors conducted scientific analysis and trials of the aspirin powder Hoffmann had created, often taking the grains themselves, to ensure that the side effects associated with taking pure salicylic acid were reduced or eradicated. After doctors had written articles for medical journals about the benefits of aspirin it became more widely used, mainly for pain relief.

Aspirin Today

In recent years, with the increase of heart disease and stroke, it has been found that aspirin is capable of reducing the incidence of blood clots in blood vessels, which in turn reduces the chance of heart attack and stroke. In some cases, doctors are prescribing low-dose aspirin be taken daily by people at risk of heart disease.

HOW ASPIRIN CAN HELP

Biomedical scientists have discovered that aspirin prevents the body from producing prostaglandin thromboxane, which aids the formation of blood clots. Blood clots can obstruct major blood vessels.

an aspirin advertisement from 1917

BAYER

One Real Aspirin

Counterfeits and substitutes may be ineffective, and even harmful. Refuse them. Protect yourself by demanding

Bayer-Tablets of Aspirin

Every tablet and every package of genuine Aspirin bears

"The Bayer Cross

Your Guarantee of Purity"

Pocket Boxes of 12, Bottles of 24 and Bottles of 100

The trade-mark "Aspirin" (Reg. U. S. Pat. Office) is a guarantee that the monoaceticacid... of salicylicacid in these tablets is of the reliable Bayer manufacture.

Migraines, Névralgies, Rhumatismes

Demandez à votre Pharmacien

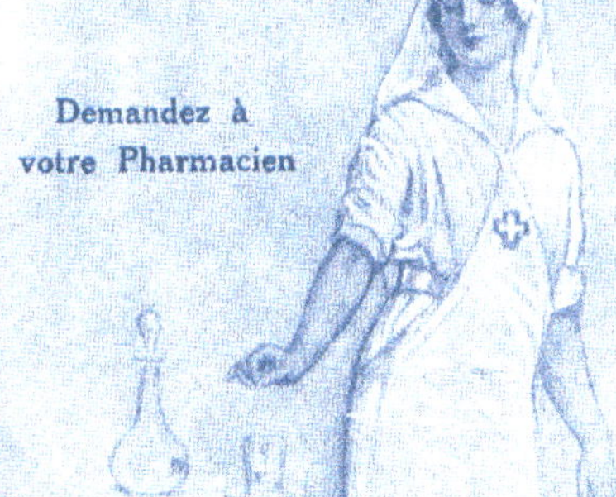

a French advertisement for aspirin from 1923

l'Aspirine "USINES du RHÔNE"

En TUBES de 20 COMPRIMÉS

LABORATOIRE des PRODUITS USINES du RHÔNE
21, Rue Jean Goujon, PARIS

Medicines, Late 1800s

During the late 1800s, all kinds of "wonder drugs" were being made and promises of miracle cures were commonplace. People were bombarded with advertisements, books and brochures and sent samples of drugs, too. Many physicians at the time were wary of companies advertising drugs that promised to cure all kinds of ailments. These companies were preying on the sick and the infirm. Physicians acknowledged that some drugs might help to ease the medical problems of their patients but noted caution first. Soon doctors recognised that some laboratory-produced drugs were helpful and thus began a relationship between pharmaceutical companies, the medical profession and pharmacies.

an old bottle of aspirin grains

7 Venom Makes Medicine

Early Antivenom Research

In Australia in 1928, government funding enabled a medical scientist, Charles Kellaway (1889–1952), and a small team to study snake venoms, from a medicinal point of view. In eight months they had extracted venom from 300 snakes! By 1930, the team had produced tiger snake antivenom, an antitoxin that treats poisoning caused by the snake's venom. Antivenom was first officially used to treat snake bites at the Royal Melbourne Hospital in 1931.

The eastern brown snake is the second most venomous snake in the world.

Top 25 Venomous Snakes

In Australia, there are over 100 venomous snakes, including 20 of the 25 most deadly in the world.

The Australian Venom Research Unit has based this list on the measure of venom required to cause death. The snakes in red are native to Australia.

a Cobra snake

1. Inland Taipan
2. Eastern brown snake
3. Coastal taipan
4. Tiger snake
5. Black tiger snake
6. Beaked sea snake
7. Chappell Island black tiger snake
8. Death adder
9. Gwardar
10. Spotted brown snake
11. Australian copperhead
12. Cobra (Asia)
13. Dugite
14. Papuan black snake (New Guinea)
15. Stephens' banded snake
16. Rough-scaled snake
17. King cobra (Asia)
18. Blue-bellied black snake
19. Collett's snake
20. Mulga snake
21. Red-bellied black snake
22. Small-eyed snake
23. Eastern diamond-backed rattlesnake (North America)
24. Black whip snake
25. Fer-de-lance (South America)

Snakes **Save** Lives

Since the 1930s, Australian researchers have discovered many uses for antivenom, and not just for helping victims of bites from snakes and spiders. In fact, deadly venom even has health uses! For example, when venom from certain snakes is recreated in the right form, it can improve the quality of life for people who suffer from health problems such as high blood pressure, heart disease and even cancer. This particular antivenom uses the protein from the venom of a species of South American rattlesnake. Administered in the right dosage, it has been shown to work a little like aspirin, and prevents blood clots from forming in major blood vessels. This is especially good news for people with a high risk of stroke or heart disease, both of which are caused by blood clots. Research has also shown that a small amount of snake venom, administered properly, can paralyse cancer cells and stop them from attaching to one another and multiplying.

a tiger snake

The inland taipan is the most venomous snake in the world.

Reptile Park Supplies Venom

The Australian Reptile Park, in Somersby, New South Wales, has been a popular tourist attraction since it opened in 1949. Since 1951, the Australian Reptile Park has been suppyling snake venom to a large biopharmaceutical company that uses it to produce antivenom to treat people who have been bitten by venomous snakes. The company also produces antivenom to treat people suffering from venomous spider bites.

Only Experts Milk Snakes

John Mostyn is the venom production manager at the Australian Reptile Park. He is an expert snake handler who appears fearless as he grips the tail of a deadly snake with one hand, and presses the snake's head against the side of a glass beaker with the other hand. The beaker is covered in plastic film so that the collected venom will not spill out. Within seconds, the snake's fangs latch onto the side of the beaker. This action very quickly releases around 300 milligrams of toxic venom into the beaker. That's enough to kill many people! Sometimes, the snake's vice-like grip is so strong that it is difficult to remove the beaker from its fangs.

an eastern brown snake

Sometimes, a pipette is held against a snake's fang to milk and collect the venom.

bottled samples of king brown snake venom

John Mostyn ready to milk a venomous snake

freshly collected taipan venom

Saving Lives of Snake Bite Victims

Venom captured from venomous creatures saves the lives of hundreds of victims of snake and spider bites. For example, venom extracted from brown snakes at the Australian Reptile Park produces enough antivenom to help save around 300 lives each year. The antivenom derived from tiger snake venom saves up to 75 lives annually.

a red-bellied black snake

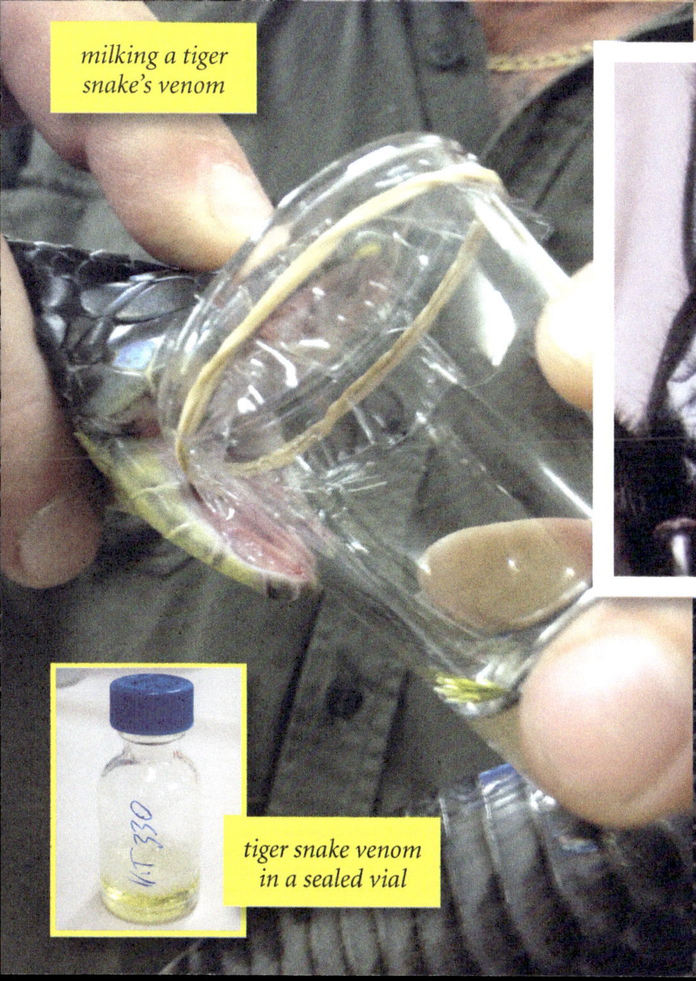

milking a tiger snake's venom

tiger snake venom in a sealed vial

Funnel-Web Spider Venom

To extract venom from a funnel-web spider, John Mostyn must first simulate the environment that will induce the spider to release venom. He does this by gently blowing on the spider or lightly touching it with forceps. In his other hand he uses a pipette attached to a suction hose to draw up tiny amounts of venom from the tips of the spider's fangs. Then he uses a special acid to flush the venom from the pipette into a vial, while keeping a watchful eye on the spider!

milking a black funnel-web spider

Leave this job to the **EXPERTS!**

Box Jellyfish **Stings**

What to Look Out For!

The bell of a box jellyfish measures up to 20 centimetres along each side. It has about 15 tentacles at each corner of its bell-shaped centre. The long tentacles, measuring about three metres, have close to 5 000 stinging cells.

Danger Zones

Box jellyfish can be found in shallow, warm shore waters when the tide is rising and at the entrance of creeks, rivers and estuaries, especially after tropical rains. They are more prevalent at certain times of the year in different parts of Australia: between October and April in the Northern Territory, and between November and March in northern Queensland and northern Western Australia.

A Lethal Injection of Venom

Box jellyfish can inject a lethal dose of venom. A person stung by the fine, trailing tentacles of box jellyfish will feel varying levels of illness and pain, depending on the size of the area that has been stung. The pain can be severe and can sometimes cause breathing trouble, so medical attention is urgently required.

First Aid for Box Jellyfish Stings

Step 1. Liberally apply household vinegar on the affected area immediately.

Step 2. Once the tentacles become inactive, they can be removed.

Step 3. A person who is confident in administering first aid may need to provide breathing assistance to the victim via mouth-to-mouth resuscitation and cardiac massage.

Step 4. Apply a pressure bandage to the affected area while transporting the victim to a hospital.

Step 5. After medical assessment, the afflicted person may require an antivenom treatment to be administered intravenously (via a drip).

8 More on Medicine

The term "medicine" is broad and encompasses many meanings: from its practice as an applied science in diverse fields of health care and medical research, through to drugs and other substances produced to prevent or treat illness. There are two main categories of manufactured medicines: prescription medicines and over-the-counter medicines.

Prescription Medicines

Only qualified medical practitioners authorised by government health authorities can advise the use of prescription medicines.

Some important things to remember:

- Read medicine labels carefully so that you know the dosage and when you should stop taking the medicine.
- Always check the use-by date as medicines can be unsafe to use or less effective after that date.
- Never share or reuse medicine.
- Store medicine at the temperature noted on the label so that it remains stable and effective.

MEDICINE MEANS?

The word has a Latin origin, and means "the art of healing". It is the root word that forms the base for many other related words, such as medicinal, medicate, medication and medical.

discussing prescription medicine with a pharmacist

a doctor handwriting a prescription for medicine

Over-the-Counter Medicine

This term refers to medicine that doesn't require a doctor's prescription. It is advisable to purchase over-the-counter medicine from a pharmacist, who is a trained health professional and can answer questions about the vast array of over-the-counter medicines and brands.

professional advice about over-the-counter medicine is available from a pharmacist

What should I do if I forget to take the medicine at the right time?

When should I take the medicine?

Ask Questions

When a doctor prescribes medicine, it is important to ask questions and seek clarification if there is anything you don't understand.

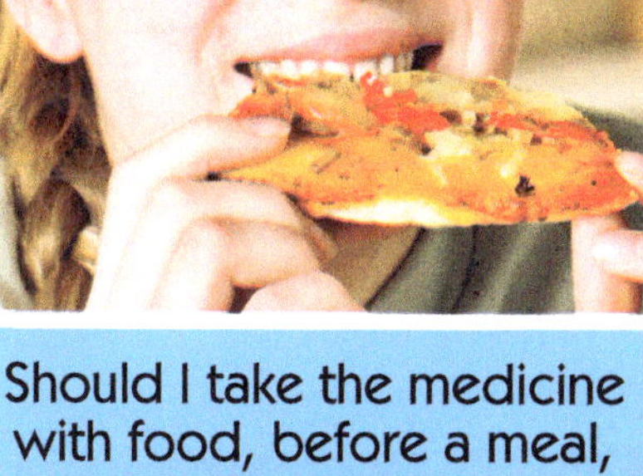

Should I take the medicine with food, before a meal, or after a meal?

How could the medicine make me feel? For example, might it make me feel tired?

If I need to take the medicine with food, how much food do I need to eat?

Index

Glossary

bacteria The simplest living organisms, some of which cause disease

beaker A glass container used in laboratories

chronic Lasting a very long time, or never stopping

culture plate A shallow dish used for growing bacteria and other microorganisms for research

fungi Kinds of living organisms including mushrooms, moulds, mildews and rusts

genus In biology, a classification or major grouping of plants or animals with similar characteristics and consisting of more than one species

mould A kind of fungus

penicillin An antibiotic agent derived from the *Penicillium* mould

pipette A narrow plastic or glass tube for measuring liquids and transferring them from one place to another

preservatives Substances or chemicals that slow down or stop the decaying process

symptoms Things wrong with the body that are signs of illness